and the Pizza Planet People

by **JOSH LEWIS**
illustrated by **STEPHEN GILPIN**

Disney · **HYPERION BOOKS**
NEW YORK

For my nephew Sam, who taught me about the
power of giant chicken nuggets, and my niece
Leah, who has to put up with Sam's talking
about stuff like giant chicken nuggets—J.L.

To my wife, Angie, who taught me that
there is absolutely nothing wrong
with chicken nuggets—S.G.

First Edition
1 3 5 7 9 10 8 6 4 2
V567-9638-5-11074
This book is set in 13-point Excelsior.

Printed in the United States of America
ISBN 978-1-4231-1500-7 (hardcover)
ISBN 978-1-4231-1535-9 (paperback)

Reinforced binding

Visit www.disneyhyperionbooks.com

1
CASCADING CRUSTS

It was a dark night. It was so dark that even things that can see perfectly fine in the dark, like cats and bats and cuttlefish, were looking around and saying, "Whoa, this is dark."

Fernando Goldberg, also known as Fern, and Lester McGregor were out in Lester's backyard playing How Long Can You Walk Around in the Dark Before You Walk into Something like a Tree or a Shed or a Swing Set?

"Ouch!" Lester shouted.

"What is it?" Fern asked.

"I tripped over a sprinkler," said Lester.

"That's another point for me!" said Fern.

"No way," said Lester.

"The game is called How Long Can You Walk Around in the Dark Before You *Walk into* Something like a Tree or a Shed or a Swing Set? I didn't *walk* into the sprinkler. I *tripped over* it."

"Same thing," said Fern.

"Not even cl—"

Lester was going to say "not even close," but before he could get the *ose* out, a supersonic speck of light, somewhere up beyond the stars, shot across the sky and then disappeared as quickly as it had arrived.

"Whoa! Did you see that?" said Lester.

"How could I miss it?" said Fern.

"What do you think it was?" Lester asked.

"Beats me," said Fern. "Probably just some kind of shooting star. Anyway, I'm winning three to one."

"Three to one?" said Lester. "That's not possible."

"You walked into the bird feeder and the side of the house and the sprinkler," said Fern.

"I told you," said Lester. "I *tripped over* the sprink—"

But before Lester could get the *ler* in "sprinkler" out of his mouth, he spotted the same light again, this time soaring along the edge of space.

Whoosh!

"That is no shooting star," said Lester.

"Yeah, maybe you're right," said Fern.

The light spiraled down into the earth's atmosphere.

"Whoa, cool," said Lester. "What do you think it is?"

At that moment, the light pushed through the clouds right above them.

"I have no idea! But whatever it is, IT'S HEADED STRAIGHT FOR US!!!" shouted Fern.

The object plunged toward the ground, right where Fern and Lester were standing.

Fern screamed, *"AAAGHHH!"*

Lester screamed, *"AAAGHHH!"*

They screamed together, *"AAAGHHH!"*

They ran every which way they could to avoid getting flattened by the whatever-it-was.

At the last second they dived into Lester's sister's Betty Beauty's Magnificent MiniMansion Playhouse.

Crash!

The mysterious missile landed in the middle of Lester's backyard.

Fern and Lester peeked at it through Betty Beauty's Magnificent MiniMansion's windows.

"Do you think it's safe to go out?" asked Lester.

"I don't know," said Fern. "But we can't stay here inside Betty Beauty's Magnificent MiniMansion for the rest of our lives."

"Why not?" Lester asked. "Look at this place. Betty sure knows how to live."

Fern threw Lester a look and started out the door. Lester followed him.

They slowly and very carefully made their way over to the object, Lester hiding behind Fern.

They inched closer.

"What if it's alive?" Lester whispered.

Fern shrugged.

They took two more steps.

"What if it's angry?" Lester whispered.

Fern shrugged again.

Three more steps.

"What if it eats us?" Lester whispered.

Fern looked down at the fallen firebomb.

"It's not going to eat us," he said. "In fact, your dog has already started eating *it*. Get away, Stanley! Get away!" Fern shouted, as he tried to push Stanley back.

"Huh?" said Lester, peeking out from behind Fern. "Whoa . . . weird . . . yum . . ."

There, on the ground in front of Fern and Lester, lay neither a rocket, a meteor, nor an alien. Nope. The thing that Fern and Lester had seen soaring through space at the speed of light was the last thing you'd expect to fall from the sky—a pizza.

But it wasn't just any pizza—it was a sixteen-inch, thick-crust pizza with a face! That's right, a pizza-topping face, with black olive eyes and anchovy eyebrows, mushroom ears, and a sausage nose.

"Cool. It's got a face just like the ones we made at Roy Clapmist's birthday party," said Lester. "Oh, but wait, where are its lips?"

"Stanley ate them," said Fern.

"Oh," said Lester as he leaned down to grab a slice.

Fern grabbed his hand.

"No!"

"What did you do that for?" Lester asked.

"Because we're not going to eat this pizza," Fern answered.

"Are you kidding me?" said Lester. "We have to. I mean, I thought I'd had pizza that was out of this world before, but this one's really from out of this world. Oh, boy!"

Lester reached for the pizza again.

"No." Again, Fern grabbed Lester's hand.

"Pizzas are meant to be eaten," Lester said.

"Not this one," said Fern.

"How do you know?" Lester asked. "Are you some kind of pizzastrologist or something?"

"No," said Fern, "I just have a feeling."

"Well, I've got a feeling too. It's called hunger," said Lester.

"Fine," said Fern. "Then go inside and order from Patty's Pizza Pantry. They deliver."

"Not from space," said Lester.

"Well, it'll have to do," said Fern.

"Earth pizza? How boring," said Lester, as he headed inside to see if his mom would let him order a pizza.

She didn't.

2

SEEKING SLICE–SISTANCE

The following day, Fern and Lester took the pizza to school in an extra-secure, reinforced, steel-plated, outer-space pizza box that Fern had created by taping cookie sheets onto a regular pizza box and adding the latch from his old Buddy Bunny's Backyard Toy Tool Shed.

During lunch they brought the pizza to the school's third grade teacher, Mr. Fennelbagel. He was obsessed with aliens and UFOs, and he knew all about this kind of stuff.

Mr. Fennelbagel looked at the extra-secure, reinforced, steel-plated, outer-space pizza box.

"So, you're telling me that you have a

pizza in there that just fell from the sky?"

"Yes," said Fern.

"Mmm . . . well, what are we waiting for?" said Mr. Fennelbagel. "Must taste heavenly! Open the box, and let's dig in!"

"That's what I said," said Lester.

"No!" said Fern.

"Why not?" asked Mr. Fennelbagel.

"You think the pizza traveled millions of light-years through space just so we could eat it?" asked Fern.

"Why not?" Lester asked. "My neighbor Mr. Dankwa gets fufu sent to him from Ghana all the time. And that's in West Africa."

"What's fufu?" asked Mr. Fennelbagel.

"It's pounded yams eaten in slimy balls without chewing," said Lester.

"Huh," said Mr. Fennelbagel. "I never knew that."

"Yup," said Lester.

"It's one thing to get fufu from Ghana and another to get pizzas from space," said Fern.

"So, are we going to eat the pizza or not?" asked Mr. Fennelbagel.

"No way," said Fern. "I thought if anyone would appreciate the importance of this pizza, it would be you."

"All right, enough is enough," said Mr. Fennelbagel. "You've had your fun, now it's time to give up the act."

"What do you mean?" asked Fern.

"You don't really expect me to believe that your pizza came from outer space, do you?" said Mr. Fennelbagel.

"But that *is* where it came from!" said Fern.

"Yeah," Lester added.

"I've spent my entire life studying the

limitless elements related to extraterrestrial activities," said Mr. Fennelbagel, "and if there's one thing I've learned through all my studies it's that pizzas come from ovens, not outer space."

"But—" Fern protested.

"No buts!" said Mr. Fennelbagel. "I'm hungry. I've wasted almost my entire lunch period listening to your ludicrous story when I could've been eating and reading my latest issue of *Little Green Man Monthly*. Now, if you'll excuse me, I've got to get to the lunchroom before lunch is over, since you're obviously not going to feed me."

Mr. Fennelbagel started for the door. "Hopefully, they still have some pizza left down there."

"Pizza day is Friday," said Lester. "It's Thursday—sloppy joe day."

Mr. Fennelbagel growled—*"Grrr"*—and walked out the door without even laying eyes on the pizza.

"What do we do now?" asked Lester.

"Good question," said Fern. "Well . . . for starters, I guess we should eat some lunch ourselves."

"Now you're talking!" said Lester.

He reached over to open the box.

"NO!" shouted Fern.

"Well, it was worth a shot," said Lester.

3

TWO PIES AND A SIDE OF GLOVES

Fern and Lester walked over to their usual table in the lunchroom carrying sloppy joes and the special pizza in the extra-secure, reinforced, steel-plated, outer-space pizza box.

"Whoa, what's that?" asked Allan Chen, pointing to the pizza box.

"It's a pizza box," said Lester.

"Why's it metal?" Allan asked.

"To keep it warm," Fern said quickly.

"What?" Lester said to Fern, confused.

"Awesome," said Roy Clapmist, reaching toward the pizza. "Can I have a slice?"

"Uh-uh, no way, not a chance," said Lester, pushing his hand away. "We're not even going to eat any."

"That's weird," said Roy. "Why do you have a pizza if you're not going to eat it?"

"Yeah," said Allan, "and if you're not going to eat it, why can't we eat it?"

"You don't get it," said Lester. "This is no ordinary pizza, it's . . ."

Fern elbowed Lester in the gut before Lester could tell Roy and Allan that the pizza came from outer space. The last thing Fern wanted was for the whole school to start freaking out about a pizza that fell from the sky.

"It's for my grandpa," said Fern.

"What?" Lester asked again.

Fern looked at Lester straight in the eye, hoping that Lester would figure out that he was lying so that Roy and Allan wouldn't find out the truth. He repeated himself slowly. "It's . . . for . . . my . . . grandpa. . . ."

Lester didn't get it. "But why would your grandpa want a pizza from outer—"

Fern stomped on Lester's foot.

"HEY!" screamed Lester.

"From outer what?" Roy asked.

"Oh," said Fern, "from, uh . . . outer . . . wear . . . emporium and . . . pizza parlor."

"Where?" Allan asked.

"You know, the Outerwear Emporium and Pizza Parlor!" said Fern. "Haven't you guys ever been there? It's awesome. They sell outerwear, like jackets and gloves, along with

pizzas and stuff. You have to go there sometime. It's the best!"

That's when Lester finally realized what
Fern was up to.

"Ohhh, yeah," said Lester. "I've been there
a million times. The last time I was there I got
a raincoat, a ski cap, and a sausage and black-
olive pizza."

"Okay, fine, whatever," said Roy, "but why
did you bring your grandpa's pizza to school?"

"Oh," said Fern, "good question. Uh . . .
well . . . um . . ."

"His grandpa's going into the hospital
today to have his elbow skin stretched, and so
Fern's bringing him his favorite pizza to cheer
him up," said Lester.

"Yeah," said Fern. "Exactly. Because it's
his right elbow, which is his favorite elbow,
so he's pretty worried. Anyway, I'm going

there straight from school, so you know . . . I brought the pizza with me and built the box to keep it warm."

"That's weird," said Roy.

"Yeah," added Allan. "Why wouldn't you just stop at the Outerwear Emporium and Pizza Parlor on the way to the hospital instead of carrying the pizza around with you all day?"

"Oh," said Fern, "um . . . because it's going to be really busy there this afternoon. . . . They're having a sale."

Lester nodded. "Free snow pants with every purchase of a large, two-topping pizza."

"Cool! I need snow pants!" said Allan.

"Yeah!" said Roy. "And I need to help you eat a large, two-topping pizza!"

"We should go there after school," said Donald "Snort" Boygle quietly to Dirk Hamstone, who was sitting beside him at the next table. "That sounds awesome." They'd been eavesdropping on the entire conversation.

"No," said Dirk. "I don't need snow pants."

"That's okay, I do," said Snort.

"The only pizza I'm eating is that one," said Dirk, pointing to Fern's pizza box. He laughed his evil little laugh.

"Oh, yeah, I get it," said Snort. *Snort! Snort! Snort!*"

Snort suddenly stopped snorting. "Wait!" he said. "Does that one come with free snow pants?"

Dirk rolled his eyes.

4
EAT AND RUN

Ms. Durbindin stood in front of her fourth grade class in the middle of the second grade hallway, holding a pebble, a grapefruit, and a rubber monkey. She was using them all as part of her bouncing unit, in which she and her students were studying what makes some things bouncier than other things, and why.

Meanwhile, up in the fourth grade hallway, Dirk and Snort were busy sneaking into Ms. Durbindin's empty classroom.

"Which desk is his?" Dirk asked, as he looked around the classroom.

Snort took in three deep snorts and said,

"That one." He pointed to a desk in the middle of the room.

"Are you sure?" Dirk asked.

"Trust me," said Snort, pointing to his nose. "This snorter could smell that pizza from a mile away."

"At least it's good for something," said Dirk.

They walked over to Fern's desk.

Dirk opened it up.

There it was—the interplanetary pizza.

Fern and Lester had done a great job of keeping the pizza with them at all times up until that point. But there was no way they could convince Ms. Durbindin to let them bring it down to the second grade hallway while she taught them about bouncing.

"*Mmmmmm* . . . pizza . . ." said Dirk, his eyes widening.

"And look!" said Snort. "It's got a face!"

"Not for long," said Dirk. "Ha-ha-ha."

He reached down and grabbed a slice.

"Whoa," he said. "Check it out, it's a pizza on top of a pizza!"

"Huh?" said Snort.

"Look," said Dirk, "there's a whole other cheese pizza hidden under this pizza. It's two pizzas in one!"

Suddenly, they heard Ms. Durbindin leading her students back upstairs to her classroom.

"Now how many of you thought the grapefruit would bounce higher than the rubber monkey?" Ms. Durbindin's voice echoed in the stairwell.

"I did," said one girl.

"We better eat fast!" said Snort.

"What do you mean, *we*?" Dirk asked.

"I thought . . ." said Snort.

"Well, you thought wrong," said Dirk. "This is my pizza. Get your own."

Dirk took a bite.

Chomp!

It was delicious, unlike anything he'd ever tasted. He ferociously chomped away at it,

while Snort just looked on. Meanwhile, Ms. Durbindin's class was getting closer and closer.

"Why did you think that, Janice?" Ms. Durbindin asked, louder now.

Chomp! Chomp! Chomp! Chomp!

"Because grapes are bouncy," said Janice.

Chomp! Chomp!

"So I thought the grapefruit would be, too."

Chomp! Chomp! Chomp!

"Interesting," said Ms. Durbindin.

Chomp! Chomp! Chomp! Chomp! Chomp! Chomp!

"Grapes aren't very bouncy at all," said Lester.

Chomp!

"And they're not related to grapefruits anyway," said Roy Clapmist.

Ms. Durbindin and her class sounded close

to the top of the stairs. Dirk grabbed the last slice, stuffed it into his mouth, and ran out of the classroom with Snort on his heels. The next second, Ms. Durbindin and her class arrived back on their floor.

Dirk and Snort ran past them and down the hallway in the opposite direction, Dirk still chomping away. He had eaten the entire pizza all by himself.

When Fern got back to his desk and discovered that the pizza had disappeared, he was baffled . . . at first. Then he remembered that the pizza had traveled millions of miles to reach Earth; so it wasn't that amazing that it had somehow managed to get out of the extra-secure, reinforced, steel-plated, outer-space pizza box and escape from his desk and the classroom. Still, he was sad to see the pizza go.

***

And now, please welcome Bert Lahr Elementary School music teacher Harvey Zwerkle.

HELLO. MR. ZWERKLE HERE, TO LEAD YOU IN A SPACE PIZZA SING-ALONG. YOU KNOW, AT SOME POINT IN OUR LIVES, EACH AND EVERY ONE OF US HAS LOST SOMETHING THAT MEANT A LOT TO US. IT'S A TERRIBLE FEELING.

This song is about Fern and how he felt after that pizza went away. It's called "Where'd My Pizza Go?" and it's sung to the tune of "Do Your Ears Hang Low?"

Remember: this is a sing-along. You have to sing!

Okay, ready? And a-one, and a-two, and a-one, two, three!

> WHERE'D MY PIZZA GO?
> THAT IS WHAT I'D LIKE TO KNOW.
> DID IT UP AND SAIL AWAY
> ON ITS PUFFY PIZZA DOUGH?
> DID IT SLINK AWAY WITH EASE
> ON ITS EXTRA-GOOEY CHEESE?
> WHERE'D MY PIZ-ZA GO?

Second verse!

> WHERE'D MY PIZZA GO?
> DID IT SLIP AWAY ON SKATES?
> IS IT FLYING OVERHEAD,
> LEAKING SAUCE ON ALL THE STATES?
> IF YOU SEE IT, WILL YOU TELL IT
> THAT I'D LOVE AGAIN TO SMELL IT?
> WHERE'D MY PIZ-ZA GO?

Third verse!

WHERE'D MY PIZZA GO?
I AM STARTING TO GET SCARED.
DID IT THINK I DIDN'T LOVE IT?
DID IT THINK I DIDN'T CARE?
THERE'S NO WAY I WOULD MISTREAT IT,
ALL I WANT TO DO IS EAT IT!
WHERE'D MY PIZ-ZA GO?

Last verse!

WHERE'D MY PIZZA GO?
I MUST KNOW OR I WILL CRY,
'CUZ THERE'S NOTHING I LOVE MORE
THAN MY THICK-CRUST PIZZA PIE.
I CAN FEEL MY HEART START STOPPING
WHEN I THINK ABOUT ITS TOPPINGS.
WHERE'D MY PIZ-ZA GO?

Say what?

WHERE'D MY PIZ-ZA GO?

Give it to me!

WHERE'D MY PIZ-ZA GO?

Bring it home!

WHERE'D MY PIZ-ZA GO?

5
IN-DIRK-GESTION

Dirk felt extremely strange that evening.

"What's the matter, precious?" Mrs. Hamstone asked Dirk at dinner. "You barely even touched your chicken nuggets. You usually chomp into them like a bloodthirsty savage. Don't tell me you're starting to make nice with nuggets."

"Are you out of your mind, Mommy?" said Dirk. "Not a chance. There's nothing I love more than sinking my teeth into those annoying, no-good nuggets."

"Then what's wrong?" asked Mrs. Hamstone.

"My stomach doesn't feel right," said Dirk.

"Oh, my!" said Mrs. Hamstone. "Well, we'll take care of that. How about a nice hot-fudge-root-beer-banana-split-float-with-chocolate-chip-cookies-and-gummy-bears-on-top sundae? That ought to settle your stomach."

She looked at Principal Hamstone, who was sitting on the other side of the table and said, "MURKWOOD! Make your son Dirkwood a hot-fudge-root-beer-banana-split-float-with-chocolate-chip-cookies-and-gummy-bears-on-top sundae."

"But, dear," Principal Hamstone grumbled, "he just said his stomach doesn't feel . . ."

Mrs. Hamstone screamed at the top of her lungs, "MURRRRKWOOOOOD!"

Principal Hamstone sighed. "Yes, dear," he said as he got up from the table and headed for the refrigerator.

"No, I don't want one," said Dirk.

Mrs. Hamstone was horrified. "WHAT?" she shouted.

"I don't want one," said Dirk.

"Oh, me, oh, my!" said Mrs. Hamstone. "Oh, me, oh, my; oh, me, oh, my; oh, me, oh, my!"

Late that night, Dirk had the weirdest experience he'd ever had. He woke up and walked to the bathroom because he had an unbelievable stomachache. It felt as if a family of ferrets was flailing around in there.

He yelped and keeled over.

"Ooh! Ah! Yayayaya!"

He could feel his insides getting pushed and pulled in every direction.

"Whoa! Yo! Ho! No! No!"

He turned on the faucet and went to splash water on his face, but before he could do that, he felt something creeping up from his stomach and into his chest.

He called out, "WHAT THE—"

That's when it appeared.

He opened his mouth, and not a bit, not some, not part of, but, rather, the entire sixteen-inch pizza—followed by the entire

hidden layer—popped out of his mouth completely whole again.

All of it landed on the floor.

Dirk stared, shocked.

But that was just the beginning.

The slices from the hidden layer started sliding around until they formed a body—with

arms, legs, and stomach—while the upper pizza, the one with the face, sat on top.

Suddenly, Dirk was standing there in his bathroom across from a fully formed Pizza Person!

Go back to sleep, Dirk, he said to himself, this is all a dream.

But it wasn't a dream, and deep down, Dirk knew it; which is why he was even more freaked out when he watched the Pizza Person walk out of the bathroom, down the stairs, and out the Hamstones' front door.

6

THE MISSING MAKINGS

Pizza Day is the most exciting part of the week in the Bert Lahr Elementary School lunchroom. Why? Because the students of Bert Lahr Elementary School love pizza. In the fall, Head Chef Rick had a contest where he asked students to write about why they loved pizza so much. He put the winning answers up around the lunchroom.

Travis Lucknel, First Grade:

*I LOVE PIZZA SO MUCH.
FOR MY BIRTHDAY, I'M GOING TO
ASK THE PRESIDENT TO MAKE
IT A LAW TO EAT PIZZA ALL THE
TIME. IF HE DOESN'T, I'M GOING TO
MOVE TO ANOTHER COUNTRY.*

Valerie Semmmellll, Second Grade:

I LOVE PIZZA MORE THAN EVERYONE ELSE BECAUSE
I ASKED EVERYONE HOW MUCH THEY LOVE PIZZA AND
EVERYONE SAID THEY LOVE IT A LOT, BUT I LOVE IT A
LOT A LOT A LOT A LOT A LOT A LOT A LOT A LOT A LOT
A LOT A LOT A LOT A LOT A LOT A LOT A LOT A LOT A
LOT A LOT A LOT A LOT A LOT A LOT A LOT A LOT A LOT
A LOT A LOT A LOT A LOT A LOT A LOT A LOT A LOT A
LOT A LOT A LOT LOT A LOT A LOT A LOT A LOT A LOT
A LOT A LOT A LOT A LOT A LOT A LOT A LOT A LOT A
LOT A LOT A LOT A LOT A LOT A LOT A LOT A LOT A LOT
A LOT A LOT A LOT A LOT A LOT A LOT A LOT A LOT A
LOT A LOT A LOT A LOT A LOT A LOT A LOT A LOT A LOT
A LOT A LOT A LOT A LOT A LOT A LOT A LOT A LOT A
LOT A LOT A LOT A LOT A LOT A LOT.

Orlando Jines, Third Grade:

I LOVE PIZZA MORE THAN
ANYONE ELSE. I NAMED MY
DOG PIZZA AND MY GUINEA PIG
PIZZA, AND I CALL MY LITTLE
BROTHER PIZZA EVEN THOUGH
HIS REAL NAME IS FRANCIS.
IF YOU ASK ME, PIZZA
IS A BETTER NAME.

Texas Ishikawa, Fifth Grade:

ALL I EVER WANT TO DO IS CRY
WHEN I'M NOT EATING PIZZA,
BUT THEN MY TEARS WOULD GET
SO HIGH THEY WOULD FLOOD
THE CITY AND MAKE ALL THE
PIZZA SOGGY. SO I HOLD IN MY
TEARS SO I CAN STILL HAVE
PIZZA.

Spertle Smith, Fourth Grade:

IF PIZZA WAS AN OCEAN, I WOULD JUMP INTO IT EVEN THOUGH I CAN'T SWIM.

IF PIZZA WAS AN AIRPLANE, I'D FLY IT EVEN THOUGH I'M TOO YOUNG TO FLY A PLANE AND DON'T EVEN KNOW HOW TO FLY A PLANE.

IF PIZZA WAS A BEAR I WOULD LET IT EAT ME.

IF PIZZA WAS BRUSSELS SPROUTS I WOULD STILL EAT IT EVEN THOUGH I HATE BRUSSELS SPROUTS MORE THAN ANYTHING, BECAUSE I STILL LOVE PIZZA MORE THAN I HATE BRUSSELS SPROUTS. THE END.

Now that you know how much all of the students at Bert Lahr Elementary School love pizza, you can just imagine what it was like that Friday on Pizza Day when there wasn't any!

"ALL RIGHT! ALL RIGHT!" yelled Mr. Pummel, the gym teacher, to all of the horrified students in the lunchroom. "LET'S REMAIN CALM."

But the students couldn't remain calm. Farnsworth Yorb was so shocked to hear the news about the pizza he passed out. Two lunch ladies knelt over him in the corner trying to revive him, while second grader Finneus Washington rocked back and forth like a petrified baby, and Janice Oglie, Winnie Kinney, and Donna Wergnort hugged each other and sobbed.

"What's going on?" Fern asked Roy Clapmist

as he and Lester walked into the lunchroom and saw the pizza panic already in progress.

"Haven't you heard?" said Roy. "There's no pizza!"

"WHAT?" screamed Lester.

"You heard me," said Roy. "NO PIZZA!"

Lester put a hand on his heart and started to wobble a little.

"How could they completely run out of pizza?" Fern asked Allan Chen, while lunch ladies squirted white bread with ketchup and tried, with no success, to serve it to students.

"Beats me," said Allan.

Lester touched his hand to his forehead. "I'm burning up," he said. "I think I'm going to die."

"You can't die from not eating pizza," said Fern.

"Oh, yeah?" said Lester. "Watch me."

TWITCH

Mr. Pummel screamed at all of the frantic students, "WE MAY NOT HAVE PIZZA, BUT WE'VE GOT PLENTY OF YUMMY WILD RICE AND GREEN-BEAN-NUT SALAD! LINE ON UP! WHO'S FIRST?"

That just upset everyone more.

"This doesn't make any sense," said Fern, as he started walking toward the kitchen.

"Where are you going?" Lester asked.

"I'm going to the kitchen to try to find out what the heck is going on," said Fern.

"Cool," said Lester, following him. "I've never been in the kitchen before."

Once in the kitchen, Fern and Lester found Head Chef Rick and his assistant, Assistant Head Chef Rhonda, sitting slumped over on a couple of overturned chocolate-milk crates.

"What's going on, Head Chef Rick?" Fern asked. "What happened?"

"I'll tell you what happened," said Head Chef Rick. "Every lunchroom head chef's nightmare happened. We don't have any ingredients to make pizza with."

"How's that possible?" Fern asked.

"That's what we'd like to know," said Assistant Head Chef Rhonda.

"It's a lot cleaner back here than I expected it to be," said Lester.

"Lester . . ." said Fern.

"We just did a major cleaning last night," said Rhonda.

"Do you mind if I look around?" Lester asked. "I've never been back here before."

"Lester!" said Fern. "This is no time to—"

"Be my guest," said Rick. "It's not like you'll be getting in the way of us working."

"Sweet!" said Lester as he wandered off into the back of the kitchen.

"So, what happened to the ingredients?" Fern asked.

"They disappeared," said Head Chef Rick.

"To where?" asked Fern.

"If we knew that, they wouldn't be 'disappeared,' would they?" said Rhonda.

"Guess not," said Fern. "So someone must have taken them."

"Of course someone took them," said Rhonda.

"But who?" Fern asked. "Who would want to break into a lunchroom kitchen just to steal a bunch of pizza ingredients?"

"That's the question," said Head Chef Rick. "Who?"

Suddenly, there was a crash in the back of the kitchen, followed by a loud "YOW!"

Fern and the chefs ran to see what it was.

There on the floor, just outside the big walk-in refrigerator, Lester was lying flat on his back.

"I slipped," he said.

"No kidding," said Rhonda.

Head Chef Rick helped Lester up, and they all started back to the front of the kitchen when Fern suddenly stopped in his tracks.

"WAIT!" he said. "You said you did a major cleaning last night. . . ."

"Right," said Rhonda.

"Well, if you did a major cleaning, then your floor shouldn't be slippery."

Fern ran back to the spot where Lester had slipped. He knelt down and examined the floor closely, then placed his index finger on a tiny little spot. It was wet. Fern lifted his finger and looked at it.

Then he smelled it.

He nodded and looked at the others. "Sauce."

"Look!" said Head Chef Rick, pointing to another little drop of sauce just past the big walk-in refrigerator over by the extra-large mixer. "There's more."

"Good eyes, Head Chef Rick," said Fern. "Now we're getting somewhere."

"So, there's a little spilled sauce. So what?" said Rhonda.

"So a lot," said Fern. "Whoever stole the ingredients got a little careless and left us a little present here."

"It's not much of a present," said Rhonda. "It's not even enough to dip a breadstick into."

"It's a present because it just might lead us to the ingredients thief," said Fern.

"What?" Rhonda asked.

"The sauce will lead the way," said Head Chef Rick. "The sauce will lead the way."

7

THE SAUCE SQUAD

Fern and Lester had to wait three whole hours, through math, art, and language arts, before they could finally go follow the sauce trail. The instant school let out, they headed back down to the lunchroom kitchen and got right back on the case.

They followed the trail of sauce to the back of the lunchroom kitchen and right out the back door.

"Hey, where are you guys going?" asked Roy Clapmist, who was standing on the other side of the door, next to the teachers' parking lot. He was playing What if Your Chin

Were Your Nose? with Allan Chen.

"Nowhe—"

Fern was trying to say *nowhere*, but before he could get it out, Lester interjected, "To capture the evil ingredient thief!"

"Cool!" said Allan.

"Excellent!" said Roy. "Let me at 'em!"

They ran over and started walking alongside Fern and Lester.

"You sure you want to come along?" asked Fern. "This isn't a game. It could be very dangerous."

"That's exactly why we're coming along," said Roy. "For added muscle."

"You have to *have* muscles to *be* muscle," said Lester.

"Ha-ha!" said Roy.

"Come on!" said Allan. "Time's a-wasting."

The boys followed the sauce trail through

the teachers' parking lot and over to the basketball court, where they ran into Gerard Venvent.

"What's going on?" Gerard asked.

"Noth—"

Fern started to say *nothing*, but of course, that was hopeless, because all at once, Lester, Allan, and Roy said, "We're going to capture the evil ingredient thief!"

"Neato!" said Gerard. He joined up with them, along with first grader Donnie Brack, who'd overheard them and wanted to be in on the hunt, too.

"Hey, you guys!" Donnie called to his friends as he and Fern and Lester and every-one else crossed the kickball fields. "Come on! We're going to take down the evil ingredient thief!"

In no time at all, Fern and Lester had

twenty-one kids following them down the trail of the secret spilled pizza sauce.

Even Janice Oglie, Winnie Kinney, and Donna Wergnort joined in, but they complained about it the whole time, of course.

"This is stupid," said Janice.

"Yeah, this is stupid," said Winnie.

"Yeah, stupid," said Donna.

The sauce trail led the kids down the big hill, onto the Ragatz Path, and right into Ragatz Woods.

By the time they came out of the other end of the Ragatz Woods and entered Ragatz Prairie, it was getting dark, but not so dark that they couldn't see something very interesting in the middle of the prairie.

"Look!" said Roy, pointing.

Sure enough, there, in the middle of the prairie, were Dirk and Snort. The group marched toward them through the prairie's shoulder-high grass.

"What are you doing here?" Dirk asked.

"We're here to stop your pathetic pizza prank," said Fern. "Where'd you put them?"

"Put what?" asked Dirk.

"The ingredients," said Fern.

"Yeah," said Lester and then Roy and then Allan and then Gerard and Donnie and Janice and Winnie and Donna and fourteen other kids.

"I don't know what you're talking about," said Dirk.

"Me, neither," said Snort.

"We're just out here spray-painting squirrels," said Dirk, holding up a spray-paint can.

"Then why aren't any of them spray-painted?" Lester asked.

"They're too fast," said Snort. "But if you look around you'll find a purple wild turkey. *Snort. Snort.*"

"He's telling the truth," said Farnsworth Yorb from the back of the pack. "I can see it from here. All the other turkeys are running away from it."

"We followed your sauce trail all the way from school," said Fern, "and it led us here."

"What sauce trail?" Dirk asked.

"This sauce trail," said Lester, pointing down at the ground.

"Oh, and look, it continues," said Roy. He charged forward through the shoulder-high grass.

"We know you stole those ingredients," said Fern.

"You don't know anything," said Dirk.

"Hey, look what I found," Roy called out. "A whole bunch of ingredients! Wonder how they got here?"

Everyone ran to Roy, who was standing in a clearing surrounded by boxes and bags and buckets of ingredients. A little wagon was parked beside them.

"We didn't steal those ingredients," said Dirk.

"Oh, yeah? Prove it," said Fern.

"I don't have to prove anything," said Dirk. "My dad's the principal of the school."

"You're dad may be principal of the school, but stealing is against the law, and he can't keep you out of jail," said Fern. "Let's take 'em in!"

"Yeah!" shouted Lester and then Roy and then Allan and then Gerard and Donnie and

Janice and Winnie and Donna and fourteen other kids.

"Wait!" yelled Dirk, pointing up to the sky. "What in the out of this world is that?"

None of the kids looked up.

"Nice try," said Lester, "but we're not falling for that one. It's older than my great-great grandmother's great-great grandmother." He grabbed Dirk's arm.

Snort pointed up at the sky and let out a bunch of frightened snorts. *SNORT! SNORT! SNORT!*

"Give up the act," said Fern, as he grabbed Snort's shoulder. "Come on."

The kids began to drag Dirk and Snort away, but then they heard a roaring blast above them.

Everyone looked up.

For once, Dirk and Snort weren't lying.

Way up in the sky was a mysterious circle spinning its way down toward the earth.

"Another flying pizza," Fern said under his breath to Lester.

But this one was not a little flying pizza like the one that landed in Lester's yard. No, this was a GIANT flying pizza.

"Run for your lives!" screamed Lester. "It's a UFP!"

They all screamed at once—"*AAAGHH!*"— and then everyone stopped.

"Wait!" said Janice Oglie. "What's a UFP?"

"An unidentified flying pizza," said Lester.

"Oh," said Janice. Then everyone started screaming again. "*AAAAAAAGHHHHHHH!*"

"That plummeting pizza's going to pummel the prairie and all the people on it!" shouted Allan Chen.

The kids scattered and ran for cover. The

sound of the deadly nosediving dough whis-
tled through the air—wwwhizzzzzzzzzzz—as
the pizza hurtled down at a million miles a
minute.

Fern and Lester dived behind a big rock on
the edge of the prairie just in time.

"Phew!" said Lester. "I thought we were
pizza pancakes for sure!"

But then, just as the unidentified flying
pizza was about to make impact, something
astounding happened!

There was a deafening *SSCRREEEECH*, as
if five thousand cars were slamming on their
breaks at the same time. And then the unidentified flying pizza stopped. Just stopped, ten
feet above the ground.

"Now I've seen it all," said Lester.

But Lester hadn't seen anything yet. Not
even close.

8
BREAD ON ARRIVAL

A hatch at the bottom of the hovering UFP opened up, and out slid a ramp.

Then a Pizza Person appeared from out of the shoulder-high grass and walked up the ramp.

"That looks like our pizza," Lester whispered to Fern, "except now it's got a pizza body."

"It's definitely our pizza," Fern whispered back. "I'd recognize that face anywhere. It must've been hiding in the grass all along."

A bunch of Pizza People came out of the unidentified flying pizza, met their friend on the ramp, and then followed Fern and Lester's Pizza Person down into the clearing in the middle of Ragatz Prairie. They looked down at the boxes, bags, and buckets of sauce and cheese and toppings. Fern and Lester's Pizza Person then reached into a bag, pulled out a couple of red peppers, put them where his mouth should be, and let out a loud cheer. "WOO-HOO!"

Then all the other Pizza People cheered "WOO-HOO!" and danced around in celebration!

They slapped each other high fives with their pizza-slice hands and danced on their pizza-slice legs. They laughed and smiled with red pepper lips, and winked at each other with black- and green-olive eyes. They wiggled their mushroom ears and sausage noses and anchovy eyebrows, and stroked their pepperoni mustaches and beards (those who had them, that is). One even threw its round, onion-slice eyeglasses up into the air as high as it could, just for fun.

"What are they doing?" Lester whispered to Fern.

"How should I know?" Fern whispered back. "I don't exactly know a ton of Pizza People."

As the celebration died down, the Pizza

People got busy and started carrying the boxes, bags, and buckets up into the unidentified flying pizza.

All around Ragatz Prairie, the kids gasped and suppressed sobs as they watched the vital pizza ingredients disappear; they were about to be shipped off into space forever.

"What do we do?" Lester whispered to Fern. "We can't just let them run off with our pizza products like that."

"I don't think we should do anything," Fern whispered back. "Who knows what kind of powers these Pizza People possess?"

Nearby, Donnie Brack was sitting behind some bushes and panicking that he might never experience the sweet taste of a pizza pie ever again.

"Uh-oh," said Lester, noticing Donnie. "He's not in good shape."

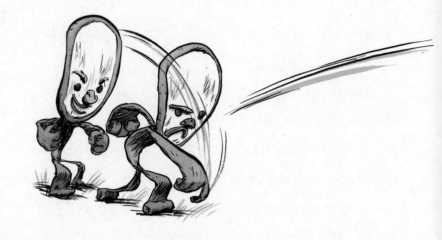

Fern looked over at Donnie. "Hey," he whispered. "Hey, Donnie."

Donnie didn't answer. He just rocked back and forth, muttering, "Must do something, must do something."

Just then, a bloodcurdling scream rang throughout the prairie. "*AAAAAGHHHHH!*"

A Pizza Person at the bottom of the ramp turned around to see Farnsworth Yorb running toward it at full speed.

It, too, screamed: *"AAAAAGHHHHH!"*
Then it reached up to one of its anchovy eyebrows, pulled it off, and flung it at Farnsworth.

Bam!

The anchovy hit Farnsworth right on the forehead and knocked him out.

The Pizza Person stood there for a moment to make sure Farnsworth no longer posed a threat, and then started back up the ramp.

Suddenly, kids started running at the

Pizza People from all around the prairie. "*AAAAAAAAGHHHHHHHH!*"

"I've got a bad feeling about this," Fern said to Lester.

When the Pizza People saw kids running at them screaming, "*AAAAAAAGHHHHHHHH!*" they screamed, "*AAAAAAAGHHHHHHHH!*" too.

And then, just like the first Pizza Person, they reached up to their pizza faces and started pulling off toppings and tossing them at the kids.

Pow!

A pepperoni pounded Allan Chen.

Thump!

A mushroom mauled Janice Oglie.

Smack!

A sausage slammed Snort!

The kids were powerless to protect themselves against the Pizza People's topping attack!

Of course, Dirk kept his distance. So much distance, in fact, that he ran all the way home to his mommy.

But not Fern; he knew exactly what he had to do as he watched his classmates dropping from toppings left and right.

"Ketchup!" he said to Lester.

"I thought you'd never ask!" said Lester.

Lester pulled a packet of ketchup out of his pocket and aimed it at Fern. "I think you're really going to like this kind," said Lester. "I got it at the Hawaiian Hamburger Hut. It's got a touch of pineapple in it."

"Just do it, already!" said Fern.

"Aye-aye, Your Chickenness," answered Lester.

He squirted his Hawaiian Hamburger Hut ketchup straight at Fern's chest, and just like that, *KERBLAM!* Fern was no longer your average everyday fourth grader. He was that greatest-of-great fried superheroes—SUPER CHICKEN NUGGET BOY!

"Now, if you'll excuse me," said Super Chicken Nugget Boy, "I've got some pizza to pulverize!"

9

TOPPING ATTACK!

Super Chicken Nugget Boy ran into the middle of the prairie shouting, "The pizza party's over, people! Time for some good old-fashioned deep-fried justice!"

The kids, battered and bruised, cheered the Breaded One's arrival.

"Super Chicken Nugget Boy!" cried Winnie Kinney. "Thank goodness you're here!"

"Just let me at those no-*dough*-gooders!" shouted Super Chicken Nugget Boy.

The Pizza People started frantically flinging toppings at him.

Whizz! Pow!

A piece of red pepper plowed into his body.

"Whoa! Those peppers pack a punch," Super Chicken Nugget Boy said to himself. But that's not what he said to the Pizza People. To the Pizza People he said, "IS THAT THE BEST YOU GOT, SAUCE FACES?"

The Pizza People didn't like being called sauce faces in the least, so they did what any Pizza Person would do—they reached up to their faces, grabbed some more toppings, and threw them at Super Chicken Nugget Boy.

Crash! Bam! Bash!

A ton of toppings trounced Super Chicken Nugget Boy.

That sausage must be supersonic! he said to himself, as he spun around and wobbled from side to side. But he didn't let the Pizza People see that they were doing any damage.

"You cheesy chumps!" he called out to

them. "You call those toppings tough?!"

He was making the Pizza People angrier and angrier; and the angrier they got, the more toppings they tossed; and the more toppings they tossed, the more he taunted them, until his breading was barely hanging on to his body. It took every ounce of his strength just to stay standing.

As for the Pizza People, they'd taken nearly all of the toppings off their faces and thrown them at him. All but the olives were gone.

"YOOOOO-HOOOOO, PIZZZZZAAAAAA PPPEEEEEOOPPPPPLLLE!" Super Chicken Nugget Boy called out. "I'm still here, you doughy dunderheads!"

That did it! The Pizza People ripped the olives from their faces and hurled them at Super Chicken Nugget Boy. But the Pizza People couldn't see where they were throwing, because the olives were their eyes.

Now the Pizza People were out of top-pings and couldn't see where they were going, either!

"Go get 'em!" Super Chicken Nugget Boy shouted to all of the kids around the prairie.

The kids came running out of hiding, screaming, "*AAAAGHHHH!*" and headed straight for the Pizza People.

The Pizza People started scrambling toward the unidentified flying pizza, but they kept bumping into each other. They bashed their heads on the edge of the unidentified flying pizza's hatch and kept tumbling down its ramp.

"Attaway!" Super Chicken Nugget Boy proudly called out to the kids as they closed in on the unidentified flying pizza and all the Pizza People.

"We got 'em!" screamed Roy Clapmist.

Just then, the biggest Pizza Person reached up and grabbed his entire pizza-head, pulled it off of his pizza-slice body, and flung it like a Frisbee at the kids.

"Look out!" screamed Lester.

"Whoa, I didn't see that coming," said Super Chicken Nugget Boy.

While the kids dodged the pizza head, nearly all of the blind Pizza People finally managed to climb aboard the unidentified flying pizza.

Meanwhile, on the other side of the prairie, Fern and Lester's Pizza Person ran off into Ragatz Woods with its entire topping face intact. No one noticed though, because everyone was too busy watching the unidentified flying pizza blast off to wherever unidentified flying pizzas blast off to.

Super Chicken Nugget Boy turned to Lester. "Hmm . . ." he said, "that didn't work out exactly the way I had hoped."

"I thought it worked out great," Lester replied. "We showed 'em who's boss, and now no one around here will worry about those outer-space Pizza People ever again."

10
PIZZA PANIC

Some people are good at predicting the future. Lester isn't.

The parents of the students at Bert Lahr Elementary became so frantic when they heard about the Pizza People problem that Principal Hamstone had to call an emergency meeting the next day, a Saturday morning, no less.

"What I want to know, Principal Hamstone, is just what you intend to do to ensure the safety of our children!" yelled Mrs. Wergnort.

"Hear! Hear!" said Donnie Brack's dad, Big Donald. "What are you going to do to

protect my boy from these petrifying pizza punks?"

"I'll tell you what I'm going to do," said Principal Hamstone.

"Uh . . . uh . . ."

"You have no idea what you're going to do!" shouted Mr. Chen, Allan's dad.

"Of course I do," said Principal Hamstone.

"So, out with it!" said Reggie Sneap, brother of first grade teacher Mrs. Sneap.

"I'm going to . . ." said Principal Hamstone.

"You're going to *what*?!" shouted Mr. Chen.

"I'm going to find out who's behind this!" Principal Hamstone finally said.

"We know who's behind it!" said Mr. Yorb, Farnsworth's dad. "The Pizza People from outer space!"

"Well, that's taken care of," said Principal Hamstone.

"Is that the best you can do?" asked Mrs. Zwerkle, the wife of the music teacher.

Principal Hamstone was silent. He had no answer.

That's when Dirk, who'd been sitting in the corner snickering, made his move. He stood up on his chair, and, in a little, innocent-as-possible voice, said, "But the Pizza People from outer space aren't the only ones behind it. They had help."

"How do you know?" asked Big Donald.

"I just know," said Dirk.

"Yeah, right," said Reggie Sneap.

"*Excuuuuse me*, sir," said Mrs. Hamstone to Reggie, "but if my son says he knows, he knows."

Over on the other side of the room, Fern and Lester looked at each other, wondering what Dirk was up to this time.

"I know who helped them," said Dirk.

"Who?" Mr. Chen asked.

"Oh, jeez," said Principal Hamstone, knowing that whatever Dirk was going to say would just lead to more trouble. "Can we just—"

"MURRRRKWOOOOOD!" Mrs. Hamstone screamed at the top of her lungs.

Principal Hamstone coughed. "All right," he said to Dirk. "Who helped them?"

Dirk took a breath and then said, "Fernando Goldberg!"

Everyone in the room gasped, including Fern.

"And Lester McGregor, too," Dirk added.

"I don't believe it for a second," said Ms. Durbindin. "Not Fernando. Fern would never help an evil pizza posse terrorize our town. Neither would Lester."

"Oh, yes, they would!" said a voice from the back of the room.

It was Mr. Fennelbagel!

"They were in my room just two days ago telling me all about their flying pizza!"

"And you didn't do anything about it?" asked Principal Hamstone.

"I thought they were pulling my leg," said Mr. Fennelbagel. "How was I supposed to know that they were planning an outer-space Pizza Person attack?"

"We came to you for help," said Fern, "because we didn't know what to do with the pizza!"

"So, you admit you have an outer-space pizza," said Reggie Sneap.

"*Had*," said Fern. "We don't have it anymore."

"GOOD GRAVY!" shouted Big Donald. "Do you mean to tell me that you had an outer-space pizza in your possession and you did absolutely nothing about it?"

"No," said Lester. "We took it to Mr. Fennelbagel."

"So, you're blaming your teacher?" said Principal Hamstone. "Have you no shame?"

"But—" said Fern.

"No buts!" said Principal Hamstone. "You've done enough damage as it is! You put our entire school, city, state, country, and PLANET at risk of complete and utter destruction! I hereby declare maximum-security detention for you both, starting immediately!"

Everyone cheered. "Yay!"

"WAIT!" shouted Mrs. Wergnort. "What's maximum-security detention?"

"I don't know," said Principal Hamstone. "I just made it up. But it's going to be bad, whatever it is!"

Everyone cheered again. "Yay!"

Principal Hamstone called out to Mr. Pummel, "Take them away!"

Dirk loved watching Mr. Pummel drag Fern and Lester away. He'd never liked them.

Of course, he didn't like anyone, but he especially didn't like *them* after their pizza gave him *extra*terrestrial indigestion. On top of that, he was furious with them for accusing him of stealing the ingredients, something that, for once, he hadn't done.

11

MAXIMUM-SECURITY SNORTENTION

Mr. Pummel set up the maximum-security detention in Mrs. Gastric's old office. Mrs. Gastric had been the school's social worker, but she found working with kids too stressful, so she went to work as a lion tamer instead.

The good thing about her office was that it was

bare and windowless, and had not one, not two, but *three* locks on the door, each with its own key. She didn't trust kids.

Mr. Pummel was so sure that his new maximum-security detention room was escape-proof that he put Snort in charge of guarding it, while he went off to play his weekly broomball game. He didn't get paid to work on Saturdays, and besides, he had the strongest wrists of anyone on his team. They needed him.

Fern and Lester sat in the maximum-security detention room across from each other while Snort sat at a desk outside. "Do you hear that?" Lester asked Fern. He was talking about the thunderous noises coming from the other side of the door.

"Yup," said Fern.

"What do you think it is?" Lester asked.

"It's Snort," said Fern. "He's snoring."

"Whoa," said Lester, "I thought it was a hippo with a jackhammer."

Suddenly, there was a knock at the door.

Fern and Lester looked at each other, confused. Why would anyone be knocking on their door when they were locked in? They couldn't open the door even if they wanted to.

"Come in," said Fern.

Nobody came in.

The boys looked at each other and shrugged.

There was another knock on the door.

"Come in," said Lester.

Still nothing.

They went to the door and listened.

They couldn't hear anything but Snort's snort-a-rific snoring.

There was another knock.

"COME IN!" Lester shouted at the top of his lungs, which scared Snort out of his slumber.

He bolted up out of his chair and started karate-chopping the air and shouting, "HO! HEY! *HIYAYA!*" until he realized that no one was attacking him.

He looked around. "What in the . . ."

"COME IN!" Lester screamed again.

Snort opened the door. "What's the big idea?" he asked. "Why do you want me to come in?"

"We don't want you to come in," said Lester. "I was talking to whoever is knocking."

"What?" Snort said.

"Somebody out there's been knocking on the door," said Lester. "So, I said to come in."

"You're crazy," said Snort. "I'm the only one who's been out here. Just me . . ." Something on the ground by the door caught his attention. ". . . And whoever dropped this off."

"What?" Fern asked.

"This pizza box right here," said Snort, as he picked it up. "Must've been dropped off by whoever you're talking about."

"Oh, yeah, now it all makes sense," said Fern. "It was my mom. She said she was going to come by with my lunch."

"Oh," said Snort.

He shoved the pizza at Fern, closed the door, locked it back up, and immediately fell back asleep.

"Thank God for your mom," Lester said as

they put the pizza box down on the ground in front of them. "I'm starving."

"My mom didn't bring this," said Fern. "She's visiting my Granny Fanny in Melton Falls."

"Then why did you say she did?" Lester asked.

"Because I'm starving, too," said Fern, "and I thought that if I told Snort she brought it especially for me, he would give it to us and not snort the whole thing up himself."

"Good thinking," said Lester. "But then, who *did* drop the pizza off?"

"I don't know," said Fern, "and I don't care. I just know that I'm *hunnggrryy*!!"

He opened the box.

"UH-OH!" he said as he looked down at the pizza.

"DOUBLE UH-OH!" said Lester.

It was the Pizza Person!

Fern grabbed the box and tried to close it, but before he could, the Pizza Person jumped up and stood in front of them.

"Wait!" said the Pizza Person. "Please!"

"What do you want from us, Pizza Man?" Fern asked.

"Help," said the Pizza Man. "I need your help."

"Help with what?" Lester asked.

"Getting ingredients," said the Pizza Man.

"You're nuts!" said Lester. "You already tried taking them once, and you saw how that turned out. Why would you ever think we'd give them to you this time around?"

"I don't know," the Pizza Man said. "But I'm desperate."

"Why do you want our ingredients so badly?" Fern asked.

"Are you kidding me?" said Lester. "Isn't it obvious? It's all part of their master plan to destroy our people and take over our planet."

"Actually, it's the opposite," said the Pizza Man. "We're just trying to save ours."

"What do you mean?" asked Fern.

"It's a long story," said the Pizza Man.

"That's okay," said Fern. "We're not going anywhere."

"Okay," said the Pizza Man. "Here goes."

12
DAWN OF THE DOUGH PEOPLE

Fern and Lester listened as the Pizza Man told the epic tale of the birth of Planet Pizza.

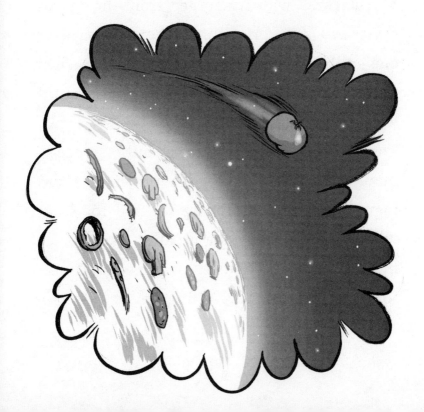

He told them of how the planet had once been nothing but a lifeless orbiting rock until one day, a klutzy astronaut, while making himself lunch, tripped on a Tri-quadrant XVX transmitter and banged into his ship's evacuation porthole. The porthole just happened to have his lunch for the day—a pizza—resting on top of it.

The pizza was discharged from the spacecraft and sent propelling through space at one million miles an hour, until it crashed with the power of fifty thousand smellowatts into what would become Planet Pizza. The pizza shattered into a billion pieces, blanketing the planet with premium pizza ingredients, and fertilizing the soil for what would soon become the greatest pizza place in the universe. Before long, a brand-new form of living, breathing pizzas began springing up from the ground.

"So, if your planet is blanketed with pre-mium pizza ingredients, why do you want ours so badly?" Fern asked.

"Because our planet is running out of those ingredients," the Pizza Man said. "For too long, the Pizza People have been too greedy and haven't cared about the future of our planet. They piled on tons and tons of unnec-essary toppings, never giving a thought to the fact that if they didn't slow down, the entire planet would run out of the very ingredients that made us in the first place."

"What are you talking about?" said Lester. "All the Pizza People we saw had plenty of toppings."

"They're not the ones we're here for," said the Pizza Man. "We're here for the Pizza Children. They're the ones who are suffering."

"How?" Fern asked.

"There aren't enough ingredients to go around," said the Pizza Man. "It's a horrible sight—young pizzas missing their little olive eyes, or their mushroom noses or rosy red pepperoni cheeks. Sometimes they'll be walking around without anything at all; nothing but bare, sauceless, cheeseless, toppingless, round pieces of dough!"

"Stop it! Just stop it!" yelled Lester. "It's horrifying just to think about it . . . and it's making me even more hungry!"

"That's why I came here," said Pizza Man. "To gather enough ingredients to make sure that the Pizza People of my planet aren't wiped out for good."

"Why didn't you just tell us all this the night you landed in my backyard?" Lester asked. "We would've helped you."

"I was going to," said Pizza Man, "but your dog ate my lips, remember?"

"Oh, yeah," said Lester. "Oops. But then, why didn't you get up and try to tell us in charades or something?"

"You try getting up and doing charades after flying through space at a million miles a minute and crashing into Earth at the end of it, and see how well you do."

"Okay," said Lester, "I get it."

"And besides, then you locked me in that extra-secure, reinforced, steel-plated, outer-space pizza box, so I couldn't have tried even if I wanted to," said Pizza Man.

"Oh, yeah," said Fern. "Gosh."

"And then, when that outer-space pizza box was finally opened again, that nasty kid Dirk ate all of me before I had any kind of chance to make a run for it," said Pizza Man.

"I *knew* he was behind this somehow," said Fern.

"So, that's when I decided to just go out and get as many toppings as I could on my own," said Pizza Man, "and then send for some Pizza People to come and get them, instead of taking the chance of getting locked up or eaten again."

Just then, muffled voices could be heard from the other side of the door.

"Someone's talking to Snort!" said Fern.

The three of them pushed their ears up against the door and stood there for a moment, trying to eavesdrop.

"It's no use," said Fern, "I can't hear a word they're saying."

"Me, neither," said Lester. "What about you, Pizza Man?"

"Nope," said Pizza Man. "Not this way. Maybe if I get my ear a little closer, though . . ."

"Good luck," said Lester. "It's already against the door. Can't get any closer than that."

"Oh, really?" said Pizza Man, as he took his left mushroom ear off and slid it under the door.

13
EARS DROPPING

"Whoa!" said Lester.

"Now I can hear them perfectly," said Pizza Man.

"What are they saying?" Fern asked.

"That annoying kid Dirk is talking about Principal Hamstone," said Pizza Man.

"What else is new?" said Lester.

"He's saying that Principal Hamstone sent out an announcement to all of the parents and teachers and students of the school," said Pizza Man.

"What did it say?" Fern asked.

"I don't know," said Pizza Man. "Oh, wait! Dirk's reading it to the snorter! It says, 'Hello, good parents and teachers and students of Bert Lahr Elementary School. First, let me say how proud I am of all of you for not going bonkers because Pizza People attacked. Although some of you did go a little bonkers, like Gerard Venvent, who built a fortress around his house using sneaker soles and straws. But just about everyone else has been incredibly brave.

"'Anyway, the good news is, you won't have to be brave for much longer, because Mr. Fennelbagel discovered what planet the Pizza People live on, and right now, as we speak, he's taking steps to make sure that the Pizza People and their planet are destroyed forever, so that they can't send any more Pizza People here to try to steal all of our ingredients and destroy us and our planet. Have a great day!'"

"Is that it?" asked Fern.

"Yeah, that's the end of the letter," said Pizza Man. "But now Dirk's saying something else to Snort."

"What?" Lester asked.

"He's saying that Mr. Fennelbagel is building a supersonic space missile to destroy Planet Pizza with," said Pizza Man.

"OH, NO!" cried Fern.

"And now he's saying that he's got a little backup of his own planned, too, just in case," said Pizza Man.

"What is it?" Fern asked.

"I don't know," said Pizza Man. "He isn't saying."

"This is bad," said Fern.

"Now he's saying, 'You'd better not screw this up, Snort!' and now he's walking away, and now the snorter is snorting and saying,

'I won't,'" said Pizza Man. "And now the snorter is starting to snore again."

— SNORE

"What do we do?" Lester asked.

"I think it's obvious what we do," said Fern. "Ketchup!"

"Um . . ." said Lester.

"Come on, time's a-wastin'!'" said Fern. "Ketchup!"

"Funny you should say that," said Lester, "because . . ."

"What?" Fern asked.

"I don't have any on me," said Lester.

"How's that possible?" said Fern. "You always have ketchup on you."

"I know," said Lester. "I don't know how it happened."

"Great!" said Fern, "Just great! Just when we need it the most, you . . ."

"Excuse me, fellas," said Pizza Man, "but while you're standing here arguing about ketchup, my planet's about to be blown to smithereens by a supersonic space missile."

"I know, Pizza Man," said Fern, "but you don't understand. Ketchup could really help you save your planet."

"That makes absolutely no sense," said Pizza Man. "But either way, WE DON'T HAVE ANY! So, can we please move on to Plan B?"

"Just relax, Pizza Man!" said Lester. "We're working on it."

"Don't tell me to relax, Ketchup Boy!" said Pizza Man.

"Whoa," said Lester. "We're just trying to help!"

"You're right," said Pizza Man. "I'm sorry. I'm just anxious about my Pizza People disappearing forever. But I'm sorry for mouthing off."

"No problem," said Lester.

"That's it!" yelled Fern.

"What's it?" asked Pizza Man.

"Mouthing off," said Fern.

"Huh?" said Lester.

"Pizza Man," said Fern, "you can hear with your ears wherever they are, right?"

"Of course," said Pizza Man.

"So, does that mean you can also talk with your mouth wherever it is?"

"Sure," said Pizza Man.

"Great," said Fern.

He grabbed Pizza Man's red-pepper lips

and flung them under the door.

They slid across the floor and landed right beneath Snort, who was once again snorting away in his sleep.

"Okay," Fern said to Pizza Man, "now what I want you to do is sound as mean and nasty as possible; in other words, sound just like Dirk, because, after all, Snort'll do anything that Dirk tells him to do."

"Wait, what? I don't get it," said Lester.

"That's okay," said Fern. "Pizza Man does. Right, Pizza Man?"

Pizza Man nodded to Fern inside the maximum-security detention room, while outside, his lips screamed, "WAKE UP, YOU SNORT-A-RONI!"

Snort leapt to his feet and started karate-chopping!

"HEE! HUH! MUMA YUMA!"

He looked around, but didn't see anyone. "Who's there?" he called out.

"WHO DO YOU THINK, YOU SNORT-WIT?" said Pizza Man's lips.

"Oh . . . hey, Dirk," said Snort. "Where are you? How come I can't see you?"

"Oh . . . hmm . . ." Pizza Man had to come up with something quick. "Um . . . I'M INVIS-IBLE!" his lips yelled. "DUH."

"Why?" Snort asked.

"Well . . ." said Pizza Man's lips, "Uh . . . it's my new strat-egy for defeating those terrible and disgusting Pizza People."

"Oh," said Snort. "Wait, I don't get it."

"It's so I can sneak up on the Pizza People if they try to steal our ingredients again!" said Pizza Man's lips. "Now, quit asking me annoying questions! We've got work to do!"

"Sure, Dirk! You got it! What do you want me to do?" Snort asked.

"First things first," said Pizza Man's lips. "Release those guys from maximum-security detention."

"What?" Snort asked. "But I thought . . ."

"When I want you to think, I'll let you know!" screamed Pizza Man's lips. "NOW, LET THEM OUT!"

"Oh, yeah, sorry, Dirk," said Snort.

He walked over to the maximum-security detention door, unlocked it, and called in to Fern and Lester. "Today's your lucky day, boys!"

"Don't tell them they're lucky!" Pizza

Man's lips shouted. "Just let them out!"

"Oh, okay, sure, sorry," said Snort. "You're free to go!"

"Really?" said Lester, as he walked out of the room followed by Fern, who was carrying the pizza box.

"Yup," said Snort.

"Awesome," said Lester.

"Now, you get in there, Snort-a-lini," said Pizza Man's lips.

"What?" Snort asked.

"You heard me!" said Pizza Man's lips.

"But Dirk . . ." said Snort.

"It's for your own good," said Pizza Man's lips. "The Pizza People are attacking again, and they're going after all snorters first. You'll be safe in there, trust me."

"Oh!" said Snort. "Thanks! I owe you one, Dirk."

He walked willingly into the maximum-security detention room.

Lester closed the door and locked it.

"Wow," said Lester, "that was the coolest thing I've ever seen!"

"Yeah," said Fern, "I might have to agree. Now, let's get out of here. We have a Pizza Planet to save!"

"You got it!" said Lester, and they sprinted down the hallway until they heard Pizza Man calling out to them.

"Hey, hey! Wait!"

Fern opened the pizza box he was holding and looked down at Pizza Man. "What's wrong?" he asked.

But Pizza Man didn't answer.

"Oops!" said Fern.

"Looks like we forgot something!" said Lester.

They ran back, got Pizza Man's lips and his left ear, and sprinted back down the hallway.

14

DURBINDIN DELIVERS

Fern, Lester, and Pizza Man headed straight for Ms. Durbindin's classroom to stock up on ketchup and grab Arnie Simpson the Salamander, just in case. But they were met with a big surprise when Lester opened his desk—there was no ketchup anywhere in sight!

"Oh, yeah," said Lester. "Now I remember why I didn't have any ketchup back in maximum-security detention. It was because there wasn't any anywhere. They ran out of all of it when they made all of those gross ketchup pizzas after Pizza Man stole the real ingredients."

"I was just trying to save my planet," said Pizza Man.

"We know," said Fern. "It's okay."

Ms. Durbindin suddenly walked into the classroom.

She screamed, "*AAGHH!*" as she saw Fern and Lester and Pizza Man standing in the middle of it.

She ran and hid behind her desk. "Please don't hurt me! I beg of you! I tried to be a good teacher to you boys, honestly I did! Please

don't sic your Pizza Person on me! Anything but the Pizza! Please, not the Pizza!"

"Relax, Ms. Durbindin, we're not going to hurt you," said Fern. "In fact, we need your help."

"My help?" Ms. Durbindin said. "Not in a million years. I would never help you and your pizza pals take over our planet. Never!"

"They don't want to take over our planet," said Fern.

"They don't?" Ms. Durbindin asked.

"No," said Fern.

"They just don't want their young pizzas walking around without faces and stuff," said Lester.

"What?" said Ms. Durbindin.

Fern, Lester, and Pizza Man told Ms. Durbindin everything—from the klutzy astronaut's lunch accident to the little Pizza Children, who were suffering because there weren't enough ingredients to go around back home.

Ms. Durbindin was crying by the end of the story. "Stop it! That's enough! What can I do to help?"

"You can tell us where they're making the supersonic space missile," said Fern.

"Of course," said Ms. Durbindin. "They're working on it in the secret gym."

"Where's the secret gym?" asked Lester.

"It's in the same place as the regular gym," said Ms. Durbindin. "They just wrote 'Secret' on the door."

"Terrific," said Fern, as he and Lester and Pizza Man sprinted for the door with Arnie safely tucked away in Fern's backpack.

"You might've just saved an entire planet of innocent Pizza People," Pizza Man called to Ms. Durbindin on his way out. "Thank you!"

15
THE SECRET GYM

Fern and Lester barged into the secret gym to find Mr. Fennelbagel hard at work on the supersonic space missile. Pizza Man hid just outside, behind

the door, so that Mr. Fennelbagel wouldn't freak out and fire the supersonic space missile at him right there in the gym. That would've been bad.

"Fernando Goldberg and Lester!" said Mr. Fennelbagel. "How in the world did you ever find the secret gym?"

"It's just the regular gym, with the word *secret* written on the door," said Fern.

"I see your point," said Mr. Fennelbagel. "But what are you doing here? I thought you were in maximum-security detention!"

"We were," said Fern, "and we were having a great time. But we just had to pull ourselves away so we could save a little pizza planet from total mass destruction."

"I see," said Mr. Fennelbagel.

"You have to stop construction on the supersonic space missile," said Fern.

"Just because you boys made friends with those crusty creeps doesn't mean that I should let them destroy us," said Mr. Fennelbagel.

"They don't want to destroy us," said Fern. "They want us to help them before they're destroyed."

"Oh, yeah, right," said Mr. Fennelbagel. "That's a good one. I haven't heard a joke that good since Mr. Hirdleman told me the one about the aardvark who thought he was a—"

Just then, Dirk walked in through the gym's back entrance.

"You escaped!" he cried out.

"That's right," said Fern.

"I knew that snortiot would screw it up," said Dirk. "How did you ever find the secret gym?"

"It's just the regular gym, with the word

secret written on the door," said Lester.

"I see your point," said Dirk. "Well, you won't be here for long. I'll see to that."

Dirk called out, "Pizza Prevention Police, report for duty!" and thirty-three Bert Lahr Elementary School students came running into the room wearing armor and carrying shields, all made out of pizza pans.

"Uh-oh," Fern said quietly.

"I second that," Lester said back to him.

"Heh-heh-heh," laughed Mr. Fennelbagel as he went back to work.

"GET 'EM!" screamed Dirk.

All of the kids started running toward Fern and Lester.

"What do we do?" Lester asked Fern.

"I don't know," said Fern. "Scream like babies?"

"Works for me," said Lester.

They both started screaming like their lives depended on it, because, well, their lives depended on it.

"HELP!" screamed Fern.

"MOMMY! DADDY! UNCLE MONTY!" screamed Lester.

The Pizza Prevention Police nearly had Fern and Lester quickly surrounded when the "secret" gym doors flew open.

"It's the Pizza People!" shouted Mr. Fennelbagel.

"Those saucy suckers!" growled Dirk.

Sure enough, twelve Pizza People came running into the room, following Pizza Man.

"How did they find the secret gym?" Finneus Washington, a Pizza Patrol officer, asked.

"It's just the regular gym," said Mr. Fennelbagel, "with the word *secret*—"

"Okay!" yelled Dirk. "We know! It's not that secret!"

Pizza Man looked over at Fern. "I thought you might need some backup!"

"You thought right," said Fern.

The Pizza Prevention Police ran toward the Pizza People.

The Pizza People grabbed toppings off their faces, just as they had in Ragatz Prairie, and

started throwing them at the Pizza Prevention Police.

But this time, their toppings did no harm. The Pizza Prevention Police's armor and shields were too strong.

The Pizza Prevention Police moved in for some serious hand-to-slice combat. They punched the Pizza People in the peppers!

"*Ouch!*"

Veggies were shattered, and crusts were crushed!

"*Ooh!*"

"Those pizza punks don't stand a chance against my Pizza Prevention Police," said Dirk to Mr. Fennelbagel, whom he had just joined up on the supersonic-missile-launching platform to watch the action.

"You got that right," said Mr. Fennelbagel.

And Dirk was right. There were just too many Pizza Prevention Police and not enough Pizza People.

The Pizza Prevention Police descended on the Pizza People like it was an all-you-can-beat pizza party.

The Pizza People couldn't even throw their toppings at the Pizza Prevention Police if they wanted to, because the Pizza Prevention Police started grabbing hold of the Pizza People's toppings themselves and ripping them off their faces and sending them soaring.

"If only I could get my hands on some ketchup, I could stop this madness and get these cowardly kids to understand that these Pizza People need protection, not punches," Fern said to Lester as he tried to pull a Pizza

Person away from Pizza Prevention policeman Gerard Venvent, who had it in a headlock.

Lester nodded as he grabbed hold of Fern's waist and helped him try to pull the Pizza Person free from Gerard.

"It's no use," said Fern, looking around at all of the defeated pizzas scattered around on the floor. "There's absolutely no ketchup to be found anywhere in this school."

Fern and Lester gave one last mighty tug.

"*AAAGHHH!*" they yelled, as they freed the Pizza Person's body from Gerard's headlock. Unfortunately, Gerard was still holding the Pizza Person's newly separated head.

Fern and Lester went flying back with the body, slid across the secret gym's floor, and crashed into their friend, Pizza Man.

Pizza Man fell backward onto the ground.

"Oh, no!" Fern said to Lester, as he looked down at Pizza Man. "He's all pale! Look!"

"That's because his sauce splattered all over you," said Lester.

"That's not good," said Fern.

"Yes, it is," said Pizza Man.

KERBLAM!

"IT'S SUPER CHICKEN NUGGET BOY AND ARNIE THE AWESOME AMPHIBIAN!" Donnie Brack suddenly screamed.

"Where?" Fern asked. Only he wasn't

Fern anymore.

He looked down at himself and discovered that he'd been transformed into Super Chicken Nugget Boy, and that Arnie had burst out of his sauce-covered backpack and turned into Arnie the Awesome Amphibian!

"Pizza sauce and ketchup must be enough alike that it transformed you guys," said Lester.

"They came to help us defeat the despicable Pizza People!" shouted Dirk.

"Hooray!" yelled all of the Pizza Prevention Police. "Hooray for Super Chicken Nugget Boy!"

Super Chicken Nugget Boy hopped on Arnie and rode him toward the center of the gym, shouting, "I'm afraid you're all wrong, you Bert Lahr barbarians. I'm here to teach you a lesson about pizza appreciation!"

"That's a good one," said Mr. Fennelbagel. "Super Chicken Nugget Boy siding with the

bad guys; now I've heard it all!"

Everyone laughed. "Ha-ha-ha!"

"I'm afraid you're the bad guys this time around," said Super Chicken Nugget Boy.

"Yeah, right. Ha-ha. Now, come on, help us finish 'em off, Super Chicken Nugget Boy!" said Allan Chen, before looking around the gym and realizing that there were no more Pizza People still on their feet, just Pizza People rolling around on the ground in agony.

Super Chicken Nugget Boy shook his head. "Nope," he said. "These Pizza People need our assistance, not our assaults."

"I think he's serious," said Donna Wergnort.

"I'm as serious as any Super Chicken Nugget Boy has ever been," said the superhero. "These Pizza People came here for our help. Their planet is running out of ingredients, and they're in danger of being destroyed. All they need is a few ingredients from us to help make their planet strong again. And besides, we don't need *all* our ingredients, do we? All we do is eat them, anyway. The Pizza People need them to see and to speak and to smile and hear. So, what do you say, gang, are you ready to help me help them get their ingredients? ARE YOU READY TO HELP ME HELP THEM SAVE THEIR PLANET?"

"He's lost his mind!" shouted Winnie Kinney.

"GET 'EM!" shouted Dirk.

"Yeah!" shouted all of the Pizza Prevention Police.

"No! Wait!" shouted Super Chicken Nugget Boy.

But they didn't wait. All thirty-three of the Pizza Prevention Police charged

Super Chicken Nugget Boy.

"Whoa, this is not the response I expected," said Super Chicken Nugget Boy. "Retreat, Arnie! Retreat!"

Super Chicken Nugget Boy rode away from the angry mob on top of Arnie.

"Give up now, Super Chicken Nugget Boy, and we'll let you off easy!" Dirk yelled.

"Yeah," said Mr. Fennelbagel. "We'll just send you to a special chicken-nugget mental hospital for the rest of your life."

"It's a sad, sad day when Super Chicken Nugget Boy becomes Super Chicken Nugget Nut," Farnworth Yorb said to Finneus Washington as the Pizza Prevention Police cornered Super Chicken Nugget Boy and Arnie over by the gym's stretching-exercise-instruction posters.

"I imagine a mental hospital wouldn't be any crazier than this school," said Super

Chicken Nugget Boy. "But still, I'm not ready to take that leap. I am, however, ready to take *this* leap! Hit it, Arnie!"

Arnie leapt back up over the surrounding Pizza Prevention Police and landed on the other side of the gym—*SQUISH*—right on top of some stray cheese that had fallen off one of the battered Pizza People's faces.

"Rats!" said Dirk.

The Pizza Prevention Police all turned and started running after Super Chicken Nugget Boy, except for Donnie Brack, who was busy running into a wall, because his eyes were covered with the cheese that had squirted out from under Arnie's feet after the jump.

"That's it, Arnie!" said Super Chicken Nugget Boy as he jumped off the Awesome Amphibian. "You go around and stomp on as much cheese as you can! I've got a plan!"

GERARD VENVENT DIVED DOWN AT THE NUGGET'S KNEES AND TRIED TO TRIP HIM UP.

I'VE GOT YOU NOW, YOU PATHETIC PROTECTOR OF PIZZAS!

PERSONALLY I PREFER PEPPERONI, BUT THIS'LL DO IN A PINCH!

GLOOP

FARNSWORTH YORB CLUTCHED A CLIMBING ROPE AND SWUNG FROM THE CEILING TOWARD THE SUPER NUGGET.

YOUR DAYS OF DEFENDING DOUGHY DUDES ARE DONE FOR!

BUT SUPER CHICKEN NUGGET BOY WAS JUST GETTING STARTED.

TWO TORPEDO TOPPINGS, COMING RIGHT UP!

I NEVER KNEW YOU HAD SO MUSH ROOM IN YOUR NOSE!

HA HA! MUSH ROOM! GET IT?

YEAH.

NOW I'M TRYING TO GET RID OF IT.

"Thanks," said Super Chicken Nugget Boy.

"Any time, Nug, any time," said Lester.

It's safe to say this was the most brutal pizza-topping battle Bert Lahr Elementary School had ever seen, especially since it had never seen one until that day.

Toppings were flying everywhere, and wherever they flew, you could be sure that there was a student on the other end getting pizzafied.

Robert Runks, known for having the biggest mouth at Bert Lahr Elementary, wasn't going to be talking out of turn any time soon. Not with two anchovies stuck across his lips, sealing them shut.

And Stan Ops, the kid who prided himself on having the best hearing in the school (and who used to say he could hear a mouse squeak in Femurtown, which was three towns away), was now struggling to hear even the loudest noises because of the slice of green pepper that he had in one ear and the pineapple slice that was lodged in the other.

And you can't forget Kritya Shankar— the Clumsy Canadian Pirate. Why clumsy? Because he had a topping slapped across one eye and was bumping into everything, and Canadian because that topping was Canadian bacon.

But perhaps the saddest sight of them all was Wendy "Rosy Cheeks" Deller, who was famous for her adorable rosy cheeks; she would now have to change her name to Wendy "Onion Cheeks" Deller.

16

PUTTING YOURSELF IN SOMEONE ELSE'S PAN

It was a pitiful scene in the secret gym that day. Humans covered in toppings were rolling around on the floor, alongside bare, topping-less Pizza People.

"There!" said Super Chicken Nugget Boy to all the kids. "Now you know what it feels like to be a Pizza Person, unable to see or to speak or to hear. It doesn't feel good, does it?"

"No," said the kids, nodding as they whimpered in guilt and pain—except, of course, for the ones with toppings in their ears, who couldn't hear what Super Chicken

Nugget Boy was saying. Lester went up to those kids personally, took the toppings out of their ears, and repeated the question to them. They agreed that it didn't feel good.

"And that's why we need to help the Pizza People!" said Super Chicken Nugget Boy. "It won't take much, just a handful of toppings from each of us, and they'll be back on their feet and good as new in no time. Is that so much to ask?"

"No," said the kids, on the verge of tears of embarrassment.

"Well, I say it is," said Dirk. "Which is why we built this supersonic space missile and why I'm going to launch it right now! Step aside, Fennelbagel!"

"But Dirk," said Mr. Fennelbagel, "I think he's got a point!"

"Don't be ridiculous!" said Dirk as he

pressed the PREPARE TO BLAST OFF button.

"NO-O-O-O-O-O-O!!!" screamed Super Chicken Nugget Boy.

"In thirty seconds, Planet Pizza will burst into a billion doughy asteroids!" said Dirk, as he wheeled the missile in its launcher over to the gym's double back doors that led out to the street. From there it had a clear path straight up to Planet Pizza!

"What now?" the kids asked Super Chicken Nugget Boy.

"I don't know," Super Chicken Nugget Boy said. "I just . . . I just . . ."

"What?" Stan Ops asked. "You've got to speak up. I've still got a bunch of pineapple in my ear."

"Of course!" said Super Chicken Nugget Boy. "The toppings!"

"TWENTY-FIVE SECONDS! Ha-ha-ha!" said Dirk, as he threw the doors open.

"Quick!" said Super Chicken Nugget Boy. "We've got to throw as many toppings as we can into that missile launcher!"

"But don't the Pizza People need the toppings?" Donnie Brack asked. "Isn't that the whole point of this?"

"Yes," said Super Chicken Nugget Boy, "in the long run. But in the short run, they have to have their planet not blow up! Now, come on!"

"Okay," said Donnie. "You're the Nugget!"

"TWENTY SECONDS!" shouted Dirk.

The kids and Pizza People—and even Mr. Fennelbagel—gathered as many toppings as they could. It wasn't so easy for the Pizza People, since most of them had thrown their olive eyes at the kids and couldn't see anymore, but they did their best.

"FIFTEEN SECONDS!" yelled Dirk. "Oh, boy, this is going to be good!"

Everyone ran to the missile launcher with their toppings.

Dirk stood guard at the missile.

"If you think I'm letting you by, you've got another think coming," he said. "TEN SECONDS! WOO-HOO!"

Super Chicken Nugget Boy grabbed Dirk and threw him across the room. He landed in a big pile of cheese and was buried up to his chin.

Everyone—the Pizza People, Mr. Fennelbagel,

the kids, even Arnie—stuffed all the toppings they could into the missile launcher as Dirk yelled at them from his cheese pile.

"It'll never work," he shouted. "That missile is way too powerful! FIVE!"

Everyone ran as far from the missile site as possible.

"FOUR!"

They dived under mats and hid behind balls.

"THREE!"

They plugged their ears.

"TWO!"

They closed their eyes.

"ONE!"

They waited for the explosion.

"ZERO!"

Blub . . .

Everyone looked up.

Blub, blub, blub . . .

Instead of a deadly missile blast, cheese and toppings slowly oozed out of the launcher.

"It worked!" shouted Lester.

"Hogwash!" said Dirk.

"YAY!" shouted the kids.

"HOORAY!" shouted the Pizza People—at least those who had lips.

"And we owe it all to Super Chicken Nugget Boy!" said Pizza Man. "Thanks, Super Chicken Nugget . . ."

Pizza Man looked around and noticed that Super Chicken Nugget Boy wasn't there.

"Hey, where'd he go?" asked Donnie Brack.

"Yeah," said Fern, who was standing at the back of the gym holding little Arnie Simpson the Salamander in his hand. "Where'd he go? That was weird."

Just then, they heard Mr. Pummel's voice

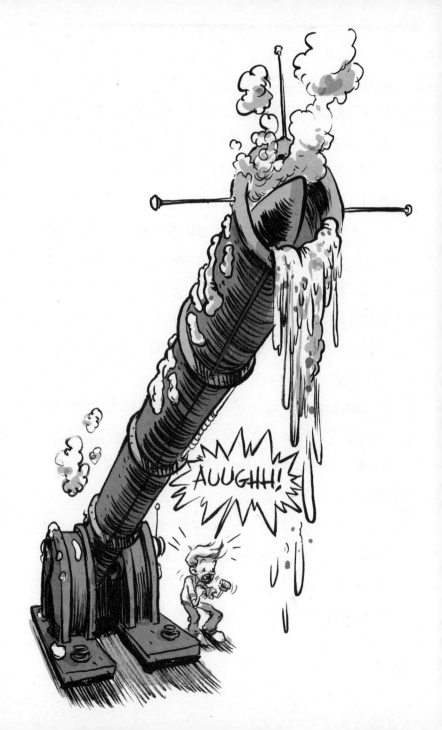

echoing down the hall. "JUST YOU WAIT UNTIL I GET AHOLD OF THOSE PUNKS!!!" he screamed. "I CAN'T BELIEVE YOU LET THEM LOCK YOU UP IN MY MAXIMUM-SECURITY DETENTION!"

"I told you," said a snort-like voice, "Dirk told me to do it when he was invisible."

"THAT'S ENOUGH OUT OF YOU, MISTER!" Mr. Pummel shouted.

"Settle down, Chuck. I'll handle this." Principal Hamstone's voice said.

Suddenly, Mr. Pummel burst through the doors in front of the gym, dragging Snort alongside him, with Principal Hamstone trailing behind.

"WHAT THE—?" said Principal Hamstone, looking around at the incredible mess of kids, Pizza People, and toppings scattered around the gym. He zeroed in on Fern. "You, my boy," he said, "are in a whole heap of trouble."

"HEAP?!" screamed Mr. Pummel. "HEAP? THAT'S PUTTING IT LIGHTLY! YOU'RE IN A HEAP OF A HEAP OF A HEAP OF—"

Bbllubb! Whhiizz! Pplloppp!

Before he could scream, "*TROUBLE*!" a huge clump of toppings burst out of the missile launcher and landed right on top of him, Snort, and Principal Hamstone.

All of the kids laughed. Mr. Pummel growled, Snort snorted, and Principal Hamstone picked out the green peppers and ate them.

"Not bad," he said.

17
SLICE OF LIFE

Once it was clear to the parents and teachers and Principal Hamstone that the Pizza People were good people who needed to be helped and not harmed, everyone in the Bert Lahr Elementary School community pulled together and lent a hand. Mrs. Wergnort provided Donna with tomatoes from their very own garden to give to the Pizza People. Roy Clapmist's Uncle Mookey, the butcher, gave Roy a terrific assortment of sausages, pepperonis, bacon, and even salamis for the Pizza People. And Lester McGregor's dad donated his prized Smurkinburgh cheese,

which he'd been keeping for a
special occasion. He figured
saving an entire planet
from destruction *was* a
special occasion.
It was a beautiful
sight to behold.

By the
time the Pizza
People were
ready to return
to their own
planet,

everyone had become the best of friends. Even Dirk and Snort had made a friend. He was a Pizza Boy with brand-new, scrunched-up green pepper eyebrows, and sardines for a mouth that was always frowning.

"I hate your planet, I'm glad I'm leaving," he said to Dirk and Snort as he and all of the other Pizza People gathered together, along with the kids, in Ragatz Prairie.

"Well, *we* hate *your* planet," Dirk said to the Pizza Boy.

"Yeah," said Snort.

"Fine," the Pizza Boy said. "So, uh . . . can I come back and visit sometime?"

"Okay,"

said Dirk, "but only if we can visit you on your stupid planet sometime."

"Fine," said the Pizza Boy.

"Fine," said Dirk and Snort.

Suddenly, from out of the clouds, the unidentified flying pizza appeared and landed in the middle of the prairie.

The Pizza People and the kids said their final farewells to one another as the Pizza People gathered all of their toppings and started up the ramp of the unidentified flying pizza.

"Well, I guess this is it," Pizza Man said to Fern and Lester.

"Yeah," said Fern. "I guess so . . ."

"Well, I don't like teary good-byes, because tears make my cheese run," said Pizza Man, "so I'll just say thanks, and if you ever find yourself running out of ingredients and losing

parts of your face, well . . . I'll be there for you, just like you were there for us."

"Thanks, Pizza Man," said Lester.

"Yeah," said Fern. "That really means a lot."

"Don't mention it. And that goes for you too, Arnie," said Pizza Man, looking down at Arnie Simpson the Salamander, whom Fern was holding.

Pizza Man reached his pizza-slice hand out to the boys, and they each shook it. Then he got on board the unidentified flying pizza, and it took off for outer space.

"Wow," Fern said to Lester as everyone watched the unidentified flying pizza disappear back into the clouds. "Things got pretty nasty there for a while. But looking around at all of us here in this prairie, I'm proud; I'm proud of how far we've come, and of how much we've learned from this experience.

And I truly believe that . . ."

Fern didn't get to finish his sentence, because Roy Clapmist and Allan Chen came running through the prairie, screaming, "LASAGNA! LASAGNA! IT'S A GIANT LASAGNA! LASAGNA! LASAGNA! IT'S A GIANT LASAGNA!"

"What are you talking about?" Lester asked them.

"There's a giant lasagna headed down Gordonville Way!" shouted Roy.

Everyone screamed, *"AAAGHHH!!!"*

"Hold on!" said Fern. "Let's all just calm down. Now, is it a good lasagna or an evil lasagna?" he asked Roy and Allan.

"Who ever heard of a good lasagna?" said Dirk.

"Well, I've never heard of an evil lasagna, either," said Fern.

"Well, now you have!" said Dirk. "COME ON! LET'S GET 'EM!"

All of the kids screamed *"AAAGHHH!!!"* and started running out of the prairie.

"What do we do now?" Lester asked Fern.

"Well," said Fern, "if he's evil, I'll have to save them, and if he's good, I'll have to save *him*. So, either way, we only have one option. Hit me with your best sh—"

Before Fern could even get the *ot* in "shot" out, Lester pulled out a packet of ketchup and squirted him and Arnie.

Kerblam!

Just like that, Super Chicken Nugget Boy and Arnie the Awesome Amphibian were back on the case!

"Whenever I think our saucy struggles are over, they pull me back in," said Super Chicken Nugget Boy, as he jumped onto Arnie's back.

He looked at Lester.

"Well, what are you waiting for?" he said, "We've got people to protect . . . or pasta to protect . . . or, well . . . I guess we'll find out when we get there."

He grabbed Lester and pulled him up to join him on Arnie's back. "Onward, you spunky salamander! Onward!" he yelled, and Arnie was off in a flash to deliver the bold, breaded morsel right back to where he belonged—at a freakish food fight desperately in need of his SUPER CHICKEN NUGGETTY JUSTICE!